Disney's

Beauty and the BEAST

Adapted by Ellen Titlebaum
Illustrated by the Disney Storybook Artists

One winter's night, a beggar woman offered a prince a red rose in return for shelter in his castle. The haughty prince sneered at her gift and turned her away.

"Do not be deceived by appearances," the beggar warned, revealing that she was really a beautiful enchantress!

The enchantress turned the prince into a hideous beast. Then she placed a spell on all the servants in the castle. She left behind only the rose she had offered him. For the spell to be broken, the prince would have to love another and earn that person's love in return before the rose's last petal fell.

4

A young woman named Belle lived in a village near the castle. Belle loved to read more than anything in the world.

Her father, Maurice, was busy working on a new invention. "You'll win first prize at the fair tomorrow," Belle predicted.

But Maurice and his horse Phillipe never made it to the fair. They got lost in the dark forest.

Black bats flew out of the shadows. Maurice gulped. Then he saw they were surrounded by a pack of wolves! The terrified horse threw his rider off his back and charged into the woods.

With the wolves snapping at his heels, Maurice ran quickly down a hillside. There, he saw a castle surrounded by a metal gate.

Maurice approached the castle and stepped inside.

"Not a word," whispered Cogsworth, the clock, to Lumiere, the candelabrum. The enchantress's spell had changed the servants in the castle into magical objects!

Friendly Lumiere announced, "Welcome, Monsieur!"

Suddenly, a huge beast stormed into the room. "A stranger!" the Beast growled.

Huge, clawed hands grabbed Maurice and dragged him to the dungeon!

At that very moment, Gaston, a local hunter, had arrived at Belle's house to propose marriage.

"Say you'll marry me," he commanded. Belle refused. There was no way she would marry that conceited bully!

Gaston left angrily. He did not like to take no for an answer.

Just then, Phillipe arrived, with no rider.

"Phillipe! Where's Papa? You must take me to him!" Belle cried.

Belle rode through the forest, braving the thick fog and frightening sounds. Soon she saw the huge turrets of the castle rising out of the mist.

Belle entered the castle and found her father locked in the dungeon. As they embraced, a voice boomed from the shadows.

"I am the master of this castle!" roared the Beast.

"Take me instead!" Belle cried.

After Belle promised to stay with the Beast forever, he released her father.

As he dragged Maurice out of the castle, the Beast called to Belle, "You can go anywhere you like . . . except the west wing. You'll join me for dinner."

The west wing was where the Beast kept the magical rose the enchantress had left. There were only a couple of petals left.

When Maurice returned to the village, he told the villagers about the horrible beast. The crowd laughed, convinced that he was crazy. This gave Gaston a wickedly clever idea. . . .

Back at the castle, the Beast waited for Belle to join him for dinner.

"Master," said Lumiere, "this girl could be the one to break the spell! You fall in love and . . ."

"She'll always see me as a monster," the Beast grumbled.

One day at dinner, the Beast remembered his manners. And later, he and Belle shared a wonderful dance. The Beast asked Belle if she was happy.

"Yes," said Belle. "If only I could see my father."

So the Beast brought Belle a magic mirror. She wished to see her father, and Maurice appeared in the glass, wandering lost in the forest.

"You must go to him. Take the mirror with you, so you can remember me," the Beast said sadly.

Belle left the castle. She found her father and brought him home. She told him about the Beast's kindness to her.

Suddenly, Gaston arrived with an angry crowd. "I'm here to take your crazy father to the asylum. He thinks he's seen a beast."

Belle had to convince everyone that her father was not crazy. She picked up the magic mirror and showed the Beast to the crowd.

Gaston locked Belle and her father in the cellar. Then he set off to attack the Beast, with the angry mob behind him.

When they entered the castle, an army of dishes and furniture assaulted them. Gaston fought free and searched the halls until he found the Beast.

At that very moment, Belle and her father escaped from the cellar and began riding toward the castle!

When Belle and her father arrived, the Beast had Gaston by the throat. "Let me go!" cried Gaston.

The Beast felt sorry for Gaston and released him.

As the Beast embraced Belle, Gaston stabbed him in the back! The Beast let out a terrible roar. Gaston tripped and fell off the balcony and was never to be seen again.

The Beast collapsed in Belle's arms.

"You came back," he said. "At least I got to see you one last time."

Belle began to cry.

In the west wing, Lumiere gasped. The last rose petal was about to fall!

"No! Please . . . please!" said Belle. "I love you!"

At Belle's words, the Beast became human once again.

"Belle, it's me," he said.

Then, the two watched in amazement as the household servants became human, too. The spell was broken at last!

Belle and her prince would live happily ever after.